Dear Parent:

Your child's love of

Every child learns to read in a different way and at his or her own speed. Some go back and forth between reading levels and read favorite books again and again. Others read through each level in order. You can help your young reader improve and become more confident by encouraging his or her own interests and abilities. From books your child reads with you to the first books he or she reads alone, there are I Can Read Books for every stage of reading:

SHARED READING
Basic language, word repetition, and whimsical illustrations, ideal for sharing with your emergent reader

BEGINNING READING
Short sentences, familiar words, and simple concepts for children eager to read on their own

READING WITH HELP
Engaging stories, longer sentences, and language play for developing readers

READING ALONE
Complex plots, challenging vocabulary, and high-interest topics for the independent reader

I Can Read Books have introduced children to the joy of reading since 1957. Featuring award-winning authors and illustrators and a fabulous cast of beloved characters, I Can Read Books set the standard for beginning readers.

A lifetime of discovery begins with the magical words **"I Can Read!"**

Visit www.icanread.com for information
on enriching your child's reading experience.

For Dad

Greenwillow Books is an imprint of HarperCollins Publishers.
I Can Read® and I Can Read Book® are trademarks of HarperCollins Publishers.

Fox Plays Ball
Copyright © 2024 by Corey R. Tabor
All rights reserved. Manufactured in Malaysia.
No part of this book may be used or reproduced in any manner whatsoever without written permission except
in the case of brief quotations embodied in critical articles and reviews. For information address HarperCollins
Children's Books, a division of HarperCollins Publishers, 195 Broadway, New York, NY 10007.
www.icanread.com

Library of Congress Control Number: 2023948815
ISBN 978-0-06-337092-0 (trade bdg.) — ISBN 978-0-06-337091-3 (pbk.)

The artist used pencil, colored pencil, and watercolor, assembled digitally, to create the illustrations for this book.
Typography by Dana Fritts
Title hand lettering by Alexandra Snowdon
24 25 26 27 28 COS 10 9 8 7 6 5 4 3 2 1
First Edition
🅖 Greenwillow Books

My First — SHARED READING

I Can Read!

FOX
Plays
BALL

Corey R. Tabor

📖 Greenwillow Books
An Imprint of HarperCollins*Publishers*

Fox is ready to play ball.

Elephant, Rabbit, and Bear

are ready to play ball.

Snail is ready to play ball too.

Fox wants to win.

Elephant, Rabbit, and Bear want to win.

And Snail?

Snail wants to win too.

Penguin blows the whistle.

Elephant kicks the ball.

Elephant kicks the ball far.

Elephant kicks the ball *very* far.

Fox chases the ball.

Elephant, Bear, and Rabbit chase the ball.

Snail chases the ball too.

Fox misses the ball.

Rabbit, Bear, and Elephant miss the ball.

Snail misses the ball too.

Fox dives for the ball.

Elephant, Rabbit, and Bear
dive for the ball.

Snail does not dive for the ball.

Hey look! Fox wins!

No . . .

"THUMP"

Elephant, Bear, and Rabbit win!

No . . .

29

Snail wins!

"Good game!" says Fox.